"Thanks to Donley, I'll have to look at my cats with a raised eyebrow from now on. Cats of the Pacific Northwest is unnerving and has visuals that will creep up your brain stem in the dead of night."

— **SHANE HAWK**, AUTHOR OF
ANOKA

"J.W. Donley coaxes you to the edge of the dark forest, through ravenous brambles and under the low brush to the black heart of the woods; the ever-hungry place that was never meant for men to see. Then he sods off and leaves you to fend for yourself."

— **MYK PILGRIM**, AUTHOR OF
A FISH DOESN'T KNOW, AND
CO-HOST OF DEADFLICKS
HORROR PODCAST

"Creepy and disquieting, CATS OF THE PACIFIC NORTHWEST is written with a sinister lyricism that seeps the story in a compelling atmosphere of horror and magic. I won't be forgetting this one soon!"

— **CASSIE DALEY,**
ILLUSTRATOR, WRITER,
PODCASTER AT LET'S GET
GALACTIC

PRAISE FOR CATS OF THE PACIFIC NORTHWEST

"This dark, contemporary fairy tale weaves together *Hansel and Gretel*, *The Blair Witch Project*, and *Get Out*, and to create an unsettling, moving, and haunting story."

— **RICHARD THOMAS**, AUTHOR OF DISINTEGRATION, AND BREAKER (THRILLER NOMINEE)

"Cats of the Pacific Northwest is a surreal journey that'll captivate you and make you follow its every word—until it's fully under your skin."

— **EVE HARMS**, AUTHOR OF *TRANSMUTED*

"Lean without sacrificing gravity and as deftly written as any King thriller, Joe's concocted a taut little neo-fairy tale that had me jealous about the creatures in my own work. I could feel the rain and hear the screams."

— **S. A. HUNT** AUTHOR OF *BURN THE DARK*

"Donley gives us a surreal, nightmarish modern fairy-tale with claws and teeth and horrific bite where no one lives happily ever after."

— **BOB PASTORELLA**, CO-HOST OF THIS IS HORROR PODCAST, AUTHOR OF *MOJO RISING* AND *THEY'RE WATCHING* (WITH MICHAEL DAVID WILSON)

"'Hansel and Gretel' meets Lovecraft's 'The Cats of Ulthar' in backwoods Washington."

— **SOLOMON FORSE**, FOUNDER OF THE HOWL SOCIETY

CATS OF THE PACIFIC NORTHWEST

J.W. DONLEY

Illustrated by
LEO CORBETT

Joe's dedication:
For my wife Melissa, who supports me through all of my crazy endeavors.

Leo's dedication:
I wish to thank my parents, Steve and Karolyn, and my brother Joe, for their continuing support and encouragement. Without them, this would not have been possible. Much thanks must also be given to the makers of the many professional materials and tools used to create these images.

CATS OF THE PACIFIC NORTHWEST

1
———

Daniel fails to find a stream after a fifth morning searching the dense forest surrounding their leaky tent. Running water leads away from the center of the Olympic Rainforest; Highway 101 and civilization waits somewhere between the mountains and the Pacific Ocean.

Emma stayed behind to conserve energy and listen for others traipsing through the backcountry. Hopefully, anyone else daring enough to trek out here during the winter season would have a functioning GPS or could at least point them back to the trail.

Daniel returns to camp, his growling stomach announcing his arrival. Emma holds a plate-sized leaf with frilled edges from the nearby undergrowth.

"Don't eat that," says Daniel. "We don't know if it's safe."

She shrugs and takes a large bite and swallows before Daniel tears the rest from her hands.

She grimaces against the taste.

"I need to eat," she says with the half-chewed leaf littering her tongue and teeth like a decade's worth of stuck spinach. "The food's been gone for four days."

"What if it's poisonous?"

Emma shrugs again, this time staring at him in defiance as he tosses the remnants of her leaf behind the tent.

Daniel worries about her thinning appearance. She was petite to begin with, eating mostly vegetarian fare and well-practiced in yoga. But now her damp clothing hangs like the Spanish moss of the surrounding forest. Her small collection of piercings and tattoos look somewhat out of place out here in the wild. After almost two weeks lost in the forest, her musculature is losing definition and she can hardly lift her hiking pack.

"Get some rest, I'll go look again for any sign of a trail or stream."

"Yes, Mr. Woodsman." Her voice is scathing. "Use those backcountry skills of yours and get us out of here." She crawls back into the tent and pulls a sleeping bag around her neck.

"You know what? We wouldn't be in this mess if you hadn't insisted we continue this little adventure without the GPS."

With a surprise surge of energy, she throws the sleeping bag aside and sits up. She jabs an accusatory finger into his chest.

"We wouldn't be in this mess if you hadn't dropped the fucking GPS! Don't you dare try and blame this on me."

She glares into his eyes, her finger still pressed into his sternum.

Daniel tries to meet her hard stare but fails. He turns away to scout the surrounding area.

2

———

The week before the trip, Daniel spent an evening bar hopping with Emma in the U-District. Daniel, a well-groomed third-year computer science major from the upper Midwest, had been dating Emma for a few months. They were celebrating another completed semester and had already developed a comfortable buzz after a few drinks at The Kraken Lounge. Emma wore her skull-patterned purple and black yoga pants and her red rain jacket over the t-shirt for one of the multitudes of local punk bands. Daniel had on his UW pullover hoodie and the pair of jeans that always seemed to get Emma pinching his butt.

En route to the next watering hole, Daniel and Emma trekked along the night streets beneath a crack wending between the tops of the U-District buildings. The neons and yellows from provocative signs and streetlights illuminated the low-hanging clouds. Scraps of fliers shorn from overcrowded lampposts littered the sidewalks. Some advertised car insurance, others, local bands playing at dives, and still others showcased a myriad of scantily clad escorts. The winter rainy season doesn't surfeit Seattle's hunger for vice.

As they approached Benny's Brewhaus, a bar hidden in a recessed storefront beneath a pile of office space and pricey condos, a pair of feral black cats darted across the sidewalk in front of them. Daniel's foot came down on one of their paws with a crunch.

The cat yowled.

"Oh, shit!" Daniel yelled. The cat turned and hissed, then swiped its claws at Daniel, hooking into his pant leg. Another growl emanated from the little black beast. It only had one eye, the empty socket weeping viscous tears down its face.

Daniel kicked his leg, attempting to fling the ferocious feline from his pant leg, then steadied himself in Emma's grasp. Finally, the cat retracted its claws and limped after its companion into a nearby alley. Hisses and spits faded as they continued to fight deep into the night.

"Poor cat. You broke its paw," said Emma, though her worry didn't seem sincere.

"Yeah. I think so. Thing just jumped out in front of me. Should we track it down and see if it's okay?"

Emma yanked on his arm to help him get away from the cat. "This town's full of feral cats. What's one less?"

This rankled Daniel, but he didn't think much of it before a raspy voice broke out from the alley.

"Nice ass." The cherry end of a burning cigarette flared in the shadows. A man, a full head taller than Daniel, stepped into the light, ogling Emma. He wore a denim jacket over a dingy white button up. His hair was thin and patchy in places, like chunks had been torn out in the past. "I can show you a good time, just gotta ditch that dud of a boy ya got there."

Emma weakly pulled on Daniel. *Did she want him to stand up for her honor? Or does she want him to avoid injury?* Daniel kept his feet firm on the sidewalk.

He'd never been in a fight, only a few playground scraps back in elementary school. He took one step in the direction Emma pulled him. Instead, she gave him a slight push back toward danger.

"You go in. Grab us a couple bar stools. I'll just be a minute," said Daniel. *There. Is that assertive enough?*

"No, let it go. Come in with me." Emma continued to tug at his arm with a lack of enthusiasm. Daniel wanted to take a stand. *That's what men are supposed to do, right?* But he also wanted to follow her into the bar and avoid a possible punch to the face. Or was he standing up for himself? It didn't matter. What would she think if he did nothing?

Emma huffed and gave him a worried peck on the cheek before heading into the pub. He thought he caught a sliver of a smile as she turned away.

Faintly, Daniel heard the hisses and violent screeching of the fighting cats rise from down the alley.

The man laughed. "What? College boy gonna give me a lesson in manners?" The man pulled a box knife from a back pocket and snicked out the blade. "I ain't got all night! Make your move, boy!"

Daniel's mouth went dry, and his tongue stuck to the roof of his mouth. He'd not considered the possibility of being stabbed in an alley. Maybe punched in the face. But stabbed? He looked over his shoulder at the entrance of the bar, a slight hope that Emma would be there to whisk him inside and away from this lunatic.

"That's what I thought. Just a pansy." The man snicked the blade back into the handle and pocketed the knife.

Daniel let out a breath he didn't realize he was holding.

"You better get in there. Wouldn't want anything to happen to that lady friend of yours, would you?"

Daniel's skin flushed as warmth bloomed up his neck and cheeks.

"I said git!" The man lunged, landing a foot only inches from Daniel's toes. He stared into Daniel's sweat-rimmed eyes for moments that stretched beyond comfort. He wanted to run. His fight-or-flight response had completely failed. He felt more like a deer in headlights. Shaking his head, the man relented and slipped down the alley, leaving Daniel to try and calm his racing heart. "And give the girl my regards." The man laughed as he returned to the shadows. It took a few minutes for Daniel to collect himself enough to move and rejoin Emma inside Benny's Brewhaus.

3

D aniel returns to camp, unsuccessful yet again. He slumps down before the tent and listens to Emma snore within. The rain resumes, pattering the canvas. Everything is wet: wet clothes against clammy skin, wet sleeping bags getting heavier as they absorb more water. He dreads a trickle of idle thoughts, adding to his anxiety. If he hadn't been so clumsy with the GPS, they'd be back in Seattle spending night after night in each other's studio apartments, him trying to work up the nerve to ask her to move in —she already kept a toothbrush in his bathroom. *If only that were the most pressing issue.*

4

"Well. What happened?" Emma asked when Daniel entered the bar. She'd tried to drag some details about Daniel's adventure in the alley, but Daniel brushed it off.

"It was nothing. He ran off once he realized I was sticking around."

Emma's smile flattened a bit as she processed his lie.

"So, how'd you do on the psych final?" Daniel redirected their conversation amongst the raucous crowd surrounding them inside the bar.

"D for degree, am I right?" Emma said and took a long draw from a fresh bottle of domestic. Her cheeks were extra rosy already.

"Damn right," said Daniel, clanking his bottle against hers with a goofy grin spreading across his face. *Crisis averted.*

Emma sat her beer on the bar and placed her hands on Daniel's thigh. "I have an idea. How about tomorrow, you and me, we go backpacking!"

Daniel's goofy grin faded. "In winter? Where you thinking?"

"I've always wanted to overnight out on the peninsula. You in? Come on. Let's do it. You know you want some of *this* out in the woods." She used her hands to outline her torso while giving him a wink.

He couldn't disagree with a suggestion like that.

He chuckled. "I've never camped in winter. There could be wombats or weasels or wildcats out there."

"Sure, or fanged rabbits ravaging wayward wanderers. Either way, I know you'll save me from the wildebeests." She punched his shoulder.

He could build a campfire and set up camp for them. It sounded like a romantic romp. Plus they could zip their sleeping bags together.

Daniel took a long swig and wiped his beer

moistened lips with the back of his sleeve. "You know what? Let's do it. I'll rent the gear first thing the morning."

"Okay, Mr. Woodsman. Do you know what gear to rent?" She clasped her hands behind Daniel's neck and pulled him close for a kiss.

"Mostly, I'm sure we'll figure it out." He leaned in to close the final gap and press his lips to hers, breathing in the evening's beer fumes of her breath.

She broke away and slapped a twenty on the counter.

"Keep the change!" she yelled over the music to the bartender filling pints at the other end of the bar. She then grabbed Daniel's hand and pulled him up from the stool.

"You're staying at my place tonight. Yours is too far," she whispered in his ear.

Just outside the brewery's entrance, Daniel halted against Emma's pulling arm. A woman stood in the window of the 50s-themed diner across the street, staring, unmoving. The yellow light of the sodium streetlamps gave her an ominous look, illumining her perfectly curled hair, the tip of a nose, and the front of a red-checkered dress.

"Is that woman staring at us?" Daniel asked with a nudge of his head.

"That? Nah. Just some mannequin they use to put pies on display in the window. You should take me there sometime. My ex brought me there for cherry pie last year. The inside gave me the creeps, though. They have a porcelain doll collection in a glass case by the register. So creepy. But really good pie."

"That mannequin is creepy enough for me. That pie better be worth it. Now, didn't we have other plans?" said Daniel, remembering Emma's promise of a night at her place.

Five stray cats sat at the base of a dumpster next to the diner, watching Daniel and Emma skip over the puddled sidewalk toward Emma's apartment. Once the couple was out of their sight, the coal-black cat in the center with only one eye returned to cleaning its shattered paw.

5

"Hey, Daniel. Wake up. Did you find anything?" Emma reaches through the tent flaps and shakes his shoulder. He'd fallen asleep seated in front of the tent in the falling mist, his neck getting extremely sore.

Daniel rubs both eyes with wet fists. "Huh? No. Nothing."

"Well, maybe I should try this time." Emma exits the tent, stirring Daniel from the remainder of his drowse.

"No! Last time you scouted, you were lost for hours. You're lucky you found me and the tent again."

"Shit! What the fuck is that?" She backs up and nearly falls over Daniel.

"What?"

"Up in that tree! There's something up there in the branches." She points with one hand while hiding her shocked gasp behind the other.

A black cat sits in a lower branch of the Douglas fir towering over their tent, cleaning one of its forepaws.

"Looks like someone's pet, I don't think there are bobcats around here, and it's too small to be a mountain lion," says Daniel. "Plus, I don't think cats are that color in the wild." It looked much like the cat he'd stepped on weeks before.

"Well, it scared me. That's the first non-plant life I've seen since we left the road. What the hell is a house cat doing way out here?"

"No clue." Daniel stands beside Emma to get a better look. Something is not quite right about the animal. He squints to try and get a clearer view, one that his brain can process. As if it senses his observation, it immediately stops its cleaning routine, and snaps its head as if looking through Daniel.

Repulsion knocks him to the ground. "Oh shit! It doesn't have a face!"

"What? What do you mean, *it doesn't have a face*? Of course, it has a face."

The cat hops to the ground, eliciting a shriek from Emma as she falls into a clump of drenched ferns behind her and tries to crab-walk backward, away from the out-of-place house pet.

"Fucking shit! It doesn't have a face," says Emma.

It has a mouth, with a full set of needle teeth and a bubble-gum tongue, but black fur covers the remainder of what would be a face—no nose, two sunken furry depressions instead of eyes.

A lack of eyes doesn't hinder its awareness of them. It looks directly at both of them with the curiosity of a predator, causing Daniel's stomach to stir, even though there shouldn't be anything in there to stir.

Emma returns to Daniel's side, and they both try and back away. The cat weaves through their legs, purring and pressing its wet fur against their rain-soaked pants, marking them as its own. Daniel pulls Emma into his arms and feels both her and the cat reverberate against him. He wonders if Emma's shivers are from the cold, the hunger, or the shock of confronting the faceless cat.

Emma screams and Daniel nearly falls backward again in horror at the sight of a second cat: an orange tabby. The tabby stalks toward them. It stops at their feet. This cat has a human face held in place by a number of rusting staples around the edges of the human skin. The staples hold the face tight over the furry, uneven surface as it looks up at Daniel and Emma through empty eyes; little orange tufts of fur protrude between the flaps of eyelids.

Daniel cannot stop staring at the skin unnaturally shifting over the front of the feline skull as it worked its mouth and turned its head as if it could see the surroundings. *This can't be real.*

The black cat continues to circle from a distance, weaving in and out of the surrounding trees and brush.

"Hungry?" The orange tabby—still seated on its haunches on the ground before Daniel and Emma—tilts its head to one side.

"It talks!" Emma cries, moving behind Daniel and gripping his pack.

"The cat talks?" Daniel replies. "Are we hallucinating?" *Am I having a nightmare?* Daniel's stomach growls, reminding him of the reality that they will both starve if they do not find food. The black cat yowls in response as it continues its stalking in the nearby ferns.

The tabby's loose eyelids blink twice. "Follow," it says before bounding out of the small clearing and into the trees, the black cat trailing.

6
____

Daniel doesn't know why they decided to follow the cats. Maybe it was the way his stomach rumbled at the suggestion of food. Or maybe he has lost his mind. If it turns out this is not a hallucination, he figures he can handle two house cats. So, they quickly donned their packs and followed the cats away from their campsite; the forest swallowed them whole.

There is no path, only a continuous carpet of rotting leaves with occasional underbrush. Where older trees had blown down decades before, young trees grow plentiful and dense. Daniel pushes through the mesh of growth; the branches press the frigid, damp layers of clothing against his skin. Emma, who is wirier, only needs to turn sideways to slip through the small gaps. The human-faced cat sits on a nearby downed tree and cleans itself while waiting for them to catch up.

Even when the rain stops, droplets continue to fall from the infinite canopy, branches, and parasitic sword ferns, soaking through Daniel's expensive waterproof and warmth layers. He is tired of being cold and wet and is less sure-footed from prolonged hunger. Emma remains quiet and her grip on his pack loosens as they pursue the cats farther.

Emma stops at a bush filled with pea-sized purple berries.

"I wouldn't eat those," says Daniel, trying to pull her along to keep up with the cats bounding over the exposed roots and bracken ahead. His own stomach rumbles as he contemplates the repercussions of eating the mystery berries.

She flings his hand away and ravenously grabs fistfuls of tiny berries and stuffs them into her mouth. Juices gush from the corners of her lips, reminding Daniel of a freshly fed vampire from a Hammer Horror flick.

"Emma! I don't know what these will do to you. Stop!" Daniel reaches for her, but she lets out a high snarl like a starved dog defending its food bowl. After a few more handfuls, Daniel grabs her shoulders and spins her around. Her angry face morphs into a scared wince as her skin flushes. She retches, leans forward, and vomits everything. A fountain of purple bile with bits of twig. He holds her shoulders as every bit of her misguided meal exits her body.

Her body shakes in exhaustion. She collapses in a fetal position next to the puddle of vomit.

Daniel kneels beside her.

"Okay, I got you. I think you're done carrying anything though," he says as he helps slip the pack from her back. He thinks about digging out everything they would need to decrease the weight, until he sees the cats. The orange tabby looks irritated.

"Follow. Now," it snarls.

"Fine. Just give us a minute," says Daniel, fully aware of how ridiculous their situation is, and now arguing with a human-faced tabby cat. "Babe, we have to keep moving. I can't carry you. Can you walk?"

Emma lies on the ground and stares blankly ahead. Daniel reaches to help her up. She snarls again, slaps his hand away, and struggles to stand on her own. Daniel watches over her, not knowing what to do. A trickle of purple dribbles from her chin as she stands and stares beyond him at the cats, wavering from side to side on the verge of collapse.

The cats lead the way once again, and Daniel offers a hand to Emma.

"Don't touch me." Her voice is weak.

"Fine. Whatever. At least let me do something." He pulls a small rope from the side of his pack and ties one end to a carabiner clip. The other he loops into a large lasso and hands it over to Emma. "We need to stay together."

She takes the lasso and secures it around her waist. He clips the carabiner to a belt loop, and they continue through the forest.

Daniel splits his focus between following the cats and making sure Emma is still on the other end of the rope. Twice she trips and pulls him down with her. He helps her up and tries to keep track of the little beasts, which no longer stop to wait for them.

7

The cats lead them to a clearing. In its center stands a small earthen hut with a thatched roof. A chimney of stacked stones belches black smoke. As the cats bound toward the hut, Daniel's stomach rumbles at... *is that roast pork?* He wants to turn and hug Emma, sure that they are saved. But she stands beside him, silent and staring, her skin sicklier than before. A crusty bit of vomit clings to her chin.

"Let's see what's cooking," says Daniel, forcing a smile. "It smells amazing." He checks that the rope is still tied around Emma's waist before following the cats, keeping a slow, steady pace through the clearing's long grass and while attempting to avoid ankle twisting holes. Emma ambles behind at the end of the rope.

On the stone porch, the cats join three other felines: two chocolate-colored faceless Himalayans, and a white Persian with the freckled face of a little girl. Daniel leads Emma onto the porch. The cats stop their mingling and stare silently. Even the cats lacking faces convey a look of greed and craving. He wants to take Emma away from this nightmare, but they are lost, and Emma won't last another day without food.

He knocks on the bark-covered door frame. A woman in a clean red and white gingham dress appears, a beaming smile on her face. She stands a few inches taller than Daniel and wears a stained leather apron over her dress, which is perfectly starched and pressed. She reminds him of a 1950s sitcom mom, always smiling, hair stiff enough to hold curls in a windstorm.

"Hello! Come in! The little rascals told me you were coming," she says. Her teeth gleam white against greasy red lipstick. "Grab a seat at the table, I'll bring some pie."

The smell of savory food is much stronger now. Daniel's mouth floods with saliva. He is distraught when he sees there is nothing on the table.

Inside is like a set-piece from the same sitcoms. Blue and beige tiles checker the floor, and a frilly patterned curtain hangs over a round, glassless window. He expects to see a retro-colored refrigerator or oven. Instead, a small cast-iron stove sits to one side of the room, a pipe leading to the chimney.

He helps Emma cross the dimly lit room to a table built from halved lengths of timber. It is about a body's length and has matching benches on each side. After removing his pack and setting it beside the door he unties the rope from Emma's waist, positions her in the center of a bench, and sits down beside her.

Light comes in through the open doorway and lights a portion of the floor. The rest of the hut writhes in the undulating orange glow cast from a hanging lantern as the woman sidles along the side of the table, working her way toward a set of pie servers beside the stove. Using a hand towel splotched with rusty red spattering, she opens the front of the stove and pulls out the plumpest pie Daniel had ever seen. The room floods with the scent of seasoned roast. She cuts two wedges and sets them before Daniel and Emma on shining white ceramic plates.

"The gravy is my own secret recipe," says the woman. She sits down across from them and sips at a ceramic mug. Her lipstick leaves a grease print on the rim. "Don't bother asking for it. I'll take it to the grave."

Daniel shoves forkfuls of meat pie into his mouth. Gray gravy runs down his chin, and he almost chokes on a piece of gristle while Emma weakly lifts and nibbles bits from her fork.

"Do you like it?" she asks, smiling through the steam rising from her coffee.

Daniel nods enthusiastically as he continues gorging himself until he cleans his plate. "Mind if I have some more?"

"Coming right up." She takes his plate and cuts another heaping wedge.

Daniel turns to Emma, who is only half through with her piece, "We're going to be all right now."

Some of Emma's normal color has returned, reminding him of her inebriated rosy cheeks in the U-District only weeks before. She sits her fork on the table and places a hand on top of his. "It looks like it," she says with a quiet rasp. Their eyes meet. They are going to be okay.

A few of the cats meow behind them.

"You'll be fed later, you little beasts. Now, off with you!" chides the woman waving the dripping pie server. Daniel remains focused on finishing his slice.

The woman places a new slice of steaming meat pie before Daniel.

Daniel points a thumb over his shoulder toward the door behind him, "What's with the cats?"

"Oh, never mind them," she says with a small wave of her hand, as if brushing away something unimportant, like a buzzing fly. "I haven't had news in a while. Who's president now?" She props her head on her palms and anxiously awaits some juicy gossip.

"You've been out here a long time, haven't you?" says Emma, her voice still weak, but improving.

"The Russians, they still causing problems?"

"I don't think so," says Daniel between bites.

"Damn. I was hoping for a bit more than that. Well, the two of you probably won't last long." The woman giggles before getting up from the table. "That little freckled girl didn't know much either. Too bad. She was a cutie."

Daniel freezes with the fork at his lips.

"Oh, I let a bit of my secret recipe slip!" She covers her smirk with a hand. "You two eat up. I'll be back to chat more after I get some work done around the outside. Maybe when I return, you can convince me to keep you around. Oh, and don't run off, sweeties. Folks are never in great shape after the cats drag them back." The door bangs behind her as she leaves the hut.

Daniel drops his fork and grabs Emma's hand. Her eyes are wide with terror.

"We've got to get out of here," he whispers to Emma. "Do you think you can walk?"

Emma nods as they get up from the table.

Standing at the open door, Daniel doesn't see the woman or any of the cats nearby. The sun moves behind the canopy through a haze of clouds.

"We go that way until we hit the 101. Then we can follow it north until we find help," says Daniel. "Don't let go of my hand."

They step out into the cool evening air. Daniel leaves his pack, fearing it will slow their escape.

"We just have to get beyond those trees."

They keep a slow pace, hoping to avoid attention.

They are twenty yards from the tree line when they hear the woman yell in a cheery voice, "Now where do you two love birds think you're going?"

Daniel looks at Emma, who grasps his hand hard enough that he can feel his knuckles grinding against each other. The woman isn't chasing them, and he can't see any of the cats. He visualizes house cats dragging escapees back to the hut with their jaws filled with needle teeth.

Emma gasps and cries out. After pulling his hand from her painful grip, he sees glowing yellow eyes peering at them from darkened woods.

"They're just cats. We can push through..." Daniel's reassurances die in his throat when one of the cats steps out of the shadows. It is the white Persian with the little girl's face. But it had changed. Its limbs are stretched to twice their previous length, as is its spine, which arches high. A black oily ichor drools from its teeth as it prowls toward them. Patches of rotting skin exposed between rifts in its stretched fur coat.

"Hungry," it growls. This time not a question and in a much more monstrous, low tone.

Daniel and Emma back away as more of the nightmarish cats step from the tree shadows, all stretched and dripping black oil from their maws. Most have no faces.

"I told you not to run," says the woman. She's behind them, fists on her hips, like she's scolding a couple of children.

Emma turns and swings at the woman. It impacts the woman's cheekbone with a POP, but the woman giggles as if she'd just heard the funniest thing about the neighbors next door. Tears pour down Emma's face as she looks back at Daniel with disdain. *He was supposed to protect her from the beasts of the woods, and he has failed.* She turns and runs into the forest while the woman continues a belly laugh.

Daniel tries to follow, but the girl-faced tabby leaps and buries its teeth in his calf, bringing him to his knees.

The woman approaches, still brandishing a greased-red smile, and looks down at Daniel with wild eyes.

"You two have spunk in ya, I'll give you that. And don't worry, they'll bring her back. But first I need to make sure you stay put." She reaches into a pouch in the front of her apron and pulls out a large wooden rolling pin. She swings it down hard on Daniel's head.

8

Daniel wakes on the tile floor of the hut, dried blood crusted in his hair. The metallic smell of blood floods his senses. Each heartbeat sends a throb of pain throughout his scalp. The sun has set, and the only light source is the fire in the lamp above. The woman leans over Emma's body. Emma lays along the table they'd eaten at earlier, her feet not quite reaching the end.

She is far too still.

The woman, in her starched dress and leather apron, blocks his view of Emma's face, but he can see that her chest is not rising and falling. The woman wrestles with something near Emma's head, and he hears a feline hiss.

"Hold still, Binx. You know it won't take if you don't hold still." She reaches for the nearby staple gun. She lowers it toward the table, and a succession of metallic clicks reverberates through the hut; each responded to with a low growl from Binx. Daniel wants to jump up and whisk Emma away, back to his crummy apartment down the street from the U-District's main bar drag. All he can do is watch, eyes wide, as his tears mix with his drying blood on the tile floor.

Daniel almost works up the nerve to force himself up, to do something, anything, when the woman moves to the side.

Binx, the faceless cat who had originally found them, now has a face. Emma's face, eyeless, shrunken, and pulled tight around the front of the black cat's head. Just like the orange tabby. A series of staples hold the edges of the skin in place.

Daniel loses all hope as the woman reaches for another tool, a set of iron tongs about hand's length. "Now for the tricky part." She lowers the tool toward Emma's head, his full view still obscured by the woman's body. Her shoulders work as she digs deep into the remnants of Emma's head before lifting the tongs above her hair, now wound up in pink spongy curlers. Pinched within the tongs are an ethereal blue strand of light. "Careful, careful now," the woman says to herself. The woman winds more than a foot of the strand onto the tool. "Open wide," she says to Binx, who obediently gapes his jaws. "That's it. Take it in. That should keep you running for a long while."

But Binx cannot keep it down. Binx wretches up the glowing strand onto the floor. It lands less than a foot before Daniel's face. Blue light glowing from within through a film of oily black slime. Quickly, Daniel shuts his eyes, afraid of what would happen if the woman knew he was watching.

"I warned you to hold still," she chides the cat. "That one's spoiled now! Oh well. Go and fetch Jasper, he'll be a better fit for the other fella." She sets the tongs back on the table and walks out of the hut. He listens, making sure Binx leaves as well, and after waiting an uncomfortably long time, he opens his eyes and sees, uninhibited, what she'd done to Emma. Emma's face was carefully cut away, exposing the intricacies of bloody musculature. This solidifies his paralysis.

"Oh, honey. Were you awake?" says the

woman, re-entering the hut with one of the chocolate Himalayans under her arm. "No one should have to see such things. It took a while for me to get used to it myself. Don't you worry though, the procedure should go much better for you."

The woman sets the cat down on the table beside Emma's ruined head and, just as Daniel regains enough of his voice to let out a defeated wail to accompany his tears, she brings the roller down on his head again.

9

Days later, Daniel jumps from the brush at the forest edge and onto an over-grown lawn with a feline grace. A little girl with pigtails sits in a nearby swing behind a ramshackle home, head cocked curiously. He wants to fight his excruciating hunger out of hatred for his new host-body and the woman who placed him in it, but at each thought against the cat's will Daniel feels himself fade, his soul a battery for the beast his face adorns.

Secretly, he hopes the girl will run screaming away from the chocolate Himalayan that just jumped from the forest wearing the eyeless face of a man. Hell, he wishes he and Emma had done exactly that. But the girl only stares with a concerned curiosity.

"Play?" asks Daniel, now sitting on his haunches before the girl's feet, a forced Cheshire smile and a tail flicking side to side. So far, he can only get out one word at a time through his feline mouth.

First, she seems confused at the prospect of a talking cat, but quickly she smiles and says, "You're a funny kitty," before jumping up from the swing.

The girl follows him into the woods, smiling as he purrs and leads the way.

END

BONUS STORY

THE CUTTER'S DAUGHTER

J.W. DONLEY

On his last night of bereavement leave, Benny worked on drinking himself to sleep in his battered recliner. He hated the silence, another reminder of his daughter's absence, which is why he muted the ten-o-clock news. He deserved the torturous thoughts, thoughts propagated in silence for not saving Adrianna from her murderous ex. He would've ridden up to the holding cell in Port Angeles to put a bullet in Tom Dawes's head, but he was robbed of the satisfaction. Tom had started a fight with a cell-mate, who then strangled the pipsqueak. Not so tough without a gun.

Benny kept out of Adrianna's personal life. She was an adult, twenty-two years old and supporting herself with a job down at the diner. He didn't want to drive her away, he liked her company, and he liked to think she liked his. They'd put up with each other for many years on their own. Adrianna was only seven when her mother had passed away.

Together they had moved on.

Together they had survived.

She was a good girl. Twice, she almost lost her job for using her tips to buy meals for the homeless. They would slip into the diner to beg patrons for change and extra food. She would interrupt their begging, find them a booth, and pour them a cup coffee. A few minutes later she would bring a full plate of eggs, pancakes, and sausage.

When Benny's paychecks were short, she would bring home a box or two of food from the diner that would, otherwise, have been tossed at the end of the night. She was his angel in a blue-checkered diner dress.

After high school Adrianna had a few offers for some colleges back east. She and Benny talked about it only once before she settled on staying behind. They were good for each other. They were a team.

Though, now, Benny was on his own.

In silence, the talking heads argued from both sides of the screen. Benny alternated pointing his left, then right, foot toward the ceiling from the extended footrest, blocking the left then right heads. They took turns yelling at his feet, which triggered an unexpected chuckle. Benny almost dropped his beer, as his hand hung over the edge of the recliner, but instead only splashed some down the side of the chair and onto the cracked linoleum floor.

Back on the television, the heads were laughing. He threw the half empty can at the screen, slammed the foot rest down, and rolled out of the chair.

He lumbered towards the kitchen, using the ethereal light of the television to find his way to another beer. That's when he saw the light in Adrianna's bedroom. Benny was sure he'd turned it off earlier. Looking through the length of the faux-wood-paneled 70s-chic mobile home, he noticed the curtains on the back window flutter, framed by the darkness of the hallway. He could understand forgetting to turn out the light, but he'd definitely not opened the window. Flashes of television light licked the unclean clothes strewn along the floor almost reaching the carpet of Adrianna's room. The skewed picture frames, hung along the hall, reflected fragmented bedroom light. Each was cracked except the center one: a photo of the whole family before Adrianna's mother, Benny's wife, died. The others were portraits of Adrianna, documenting her years through pre-school, grade school, and high-school, now obscured by the damaged glass.

He bypassed the kitchen, forgetting the beer, and eased towards his daughter's room. With each step he felt his heart thud a bit harder and more sweat run from his pores. The curtain continued to flutter in the draft, tantalizing him forward. Daring him to question his own wits. Was he still all there? Or, now that he was completely alone, were his faculties drifting away? Her room was the only part of the home with carpet, and when he was sober enough to stand, he made sure to vacuum. Each day the room stayed as clean as the day before.

His feet sunk into the lush carpet, eliciting a sigh of beer-tinged breath. Heart rate relaxed slightly, sweat slowed.

Adrianna's peach-colored vanity was a tableau

of any young woman's morning make-up routine. Beside it, lace curtains reached like wanting arms, lonely and missing the girl who grew up in the room at the end of the mobile home.

Glass shattered behind Benny in the hall, sending his heart racing again. He turned and saw the central photo on the floor surrounded in glass shards reflecting the flickering television light.

A familiar voice spoke from the vanity, "Hey Benny. Old man Benny. How you been?" The voice of Tom Dawes, but different. More raspy, but still cocky as ever.

Not possible, no way, Nuh-uh.

Benny turned to verify the source of the voice and was shocked to find a black cat sitting among Adrianna's makeup and barrettes; the waving curtains dropping slowly away as if wanting to distance themselves from the new intruder. Benny nearly fell to the floor, but caught himself on the door jamb, stammering for words. This was no ordinary cat; instead of having a feline face, this one had Tom Dawes's mug stretched over the front of its head, like a rubber mask pulled tight over a solid irregular surface. Staples down the sides held the skin in place. Tufts of fur and normal feline features stuck out from Tom's mouth and nostrils as he smiled up at Benny, clearly enjoying the effect of his appearance on the man.

"T-T-Tom?" Benny managed to get out, still clutching the door jamb for balance.

"I brought ya' a little present, Pops." He nudged a dead owlet forward with one paw, pushing aside a few colorful plastic bird barrettes. It then began cleaning its paw with a cat's tongue through the Tom-mask's mouth. The barrettes were meant for little girls, but Adrianna loved wearing a plastic bright-colored bird clipping her bangs to the side. She continued this habit as an adult.

"What the..."

"Fuck! I know! Great, right? Though it seems my voice box is crushed a wee bit. That big fucker strangled me real good." 'Real' came out with a rumbly growl.

"I can't handle this." Benny slumped to the floor, the impact shook the mobile home. Legs splayed out at an angle before him.

"Damn, Benny! You're puttin' on some weight.

Don't worry, I'll let you get back to drinkin' soon. I have a little tidbit I want to share with you first." Tom's snarl of a smile stretched across to both sides of the feline skull in unnatural curves and angles, stressing the staples.

Benny stared in uncomfortable silence.

This must not have been Tom's desired response. He held the smile through the quiet before blurting out in laughter, "She was going to leave you!"

Benny's eyes gained focus. "What?"

"Leave us... Well, I guess she had left me already. But her and that new schlub of hers were going to up and abandon you," said Tom.

"What the hell are you talking about?" said Benny. "What schlub? I didn't see another guy around after she dropped your ass." The alcohol slowed his speech, but he got it all out with a bit of drunken concentration, even while he plotted how to gain the satisfaction of choking the life from Tom's face.

"You didn't know Phil was shtupping your own daughter?" A fanged Cheshire smile took hold again to accent his exaggerated, insincere tone. "Tsk, tsk. And you work with him? That bastard!" Bone and sinew moved beneath Tom's grisly facade of pale freckles and two-day-growth facial hair, while he watched Benny process this new information. Benny had been training Phil as his felling partner for the past six months or so. Phil was a dependable guy, he'd even brought a casserole after the funeral, which sat untouched and rotting on the kitchen counter.

"That's why I killed her. I couldn't have her leaving me... uh, leaving us. You. All alone to rot away in this tin can." Tom hopped to the floor with a cat's grace, still holding a demented grin. Sitting on his haunches between Benny's legs he said, "She won't leave now that she's planted in the family plot."

That's when everything sunk in; sobriety peaked allowing Benny function enough to act. He dove forward, bending at the waist, trying to grab Tom, but the cat was fast. The Tom-like-cat hopped off the floor, then launched itself from the vanity out the window.

"Happy trails, Pops!" Tom Dawes yelled back as he disappeared into the night, the sound of his laughter fading down the alley.

Benny slammed the metal-framed window down hard enough to crack the single pane up the middle. *More broken glass*, he thought to himself.

He left the light on for the dead owlet on the vanity and ignored the freshly broken picture frame on the hallway floor. Instead of sleeping, he prepared himself to confront Phil on his first day back to work, then, only hours away.

There are a number of fatal accidents every year in the logging industry, and, over the remainder of the night before, Benny had decided that Phil was going to be part of those statistics.

Benny drove the rusted blue F-100 truck along the rough forestry road which wound its way up the precarious side of the Shuwan Creek valley. Rain speckled the windshield as the old wipers streaked double arcs of smeared bug guts and bird shit across his vision. He had picked up Phil at the grocery parking lot on the north end of town, just as he had done before Adrianna's death.

Phil stared out the passenger window at the higher ground passing by, ignoring the deep valley view out the driver's side. Avoiding eye contact with Benny, which only fueled Benny's intentions.

The old metal beast creaked and popped as it rumbled over the double-rutted road, nothing more than a man-made ledge cut into the side of the valley wall with the occasional pull out. The rubber rolled inches from the edge of the drop, which plummeted hundreds of feet into pristine forest valley..

Ahead, beside the road, a snag stabbed upwards marking the most precarious section of the route. Fading scorch marks from a lightning strike still decorated the outer shell of the giant cedar. A barn owl, with white ovoid face studded with coal black eyes, perched on top. It's light colors and elegant shape were stark against the harsh surroundings.

Benny thought for a moment that the owl looked directly at him, staring him down as if waiting for him to falter. Falter and be carried away in its talons, prey to feed its young. He shook the thought away and continued forward.

Washouts had forced the Kulshan Lumber Products Company to rebuild this section of road a few times over recent years. Benny slowed to an idle as he rolled through the narrow bit of road-way. The passenger mirror scraped against the bramble growing on the upward slope only inches beyond Phil's nose.

As the truck rolled past the seemingly infinite

drop to the stony valley below, Phil glanced over from the safety of the ascending valley wall. "Man, there's no coming back from a fall like that," Phil said with a nervous laugh. Quickly, he turned back to his comforting view of proximate ground. But not before Benny caught a glimpse of Phil's guilt-ridden eyes.

"Nope. You don't come back from that." Benny smirked and considered cranking the wheel and careening them both into the abyss. Maybe St. Peter would believe the road had washed out. A heavy storm had gone through the night before as he sharpened the cleats on his cork-boots in the grey television light. Besides, his hands were slick with sweat from his strangle-grip on the wheel.

But the thought of the owl staring down from above, hungering for his flesh, waiting for any fault in resolve. He felt hunted. *Do not falter,* Benny thought to himself.

Under the owl's gaze, Benny continued to inch the wheels over the narrow bit of road between tree and oblivion. Each stone and twig cracked beneath the rolling tires. Gravel and clumps of earth fell and tumbled down to the valley below. Phil maintained his vigil on the rising slope to the right while Benny stared ahead, white-knuckles steering the truck.

Inching along, Benny could see in his mind the left rim of the tires kissing the edge of the road. One slip of his hands would finish this business. But the owl watched. He could feel its visceral glare piercing the cab of the truck. He pushed forward under predator eyes.

Finally, the back tires cleared the wash-out. The owl lifted its wings and took flight into a group of uncut trees below the edge to the left. Both Benny and Phil let out sighs of relief.

One chance missed, Benny thought.

He accelerated the truck toward a small turnout on the left, only forty or fifty feet passed the empty snag. Phil turned and stared at Benny, worry and guilt flooding from Phil's trembling body as Benny slammed on the brakes, sliding rubber over loose gravel, until the truck came to a rocking stop.

Without a word, Benny killed the engine, opened his door, and swung out his legs. He pulled off his beaten up old driving sneakers and, having pulled them out from under his seat, slipped his cork boots on, careful not to let the freshly-sharpened metal cleats further scratch up the truck's side runner.

Phil trembled in silence, frozen in shock while Benny secured his laces. The sound of the wind-swayed creaking trees joined with the rumble of diesel machinery just over the next rise, amplified through the quiet around them. Rain drops pattered on the metal surfaces of the hood and roof of the cab.

Ready for business, Benny hopped out of the driver's seat and grabbed his hand axe from the truck bed. He saw the other crew truck parked fifty feet up the road in the next turnout. He could see the cables running down the slope from the skidder engine. Billows of black smoke roiled from the skidder's exhaust as Buster pulled the logs up the hill. Frankie was the usual choker-setter, a wily, bearded twig. If Buster was pulling logs, Frankie had been busy since early morning setting cables. Benny had worked with them for years, through times of both boom and bust. He mourned the end of those years. There would be no more of them after he dealt with Phil.

Benny assumed they wouldn't hear anything over the aged diesel engine of the skidder.

Thunder cracked through the terrain as

Benny circled the truck, all while staring at Phil who still sat in the passenger seat. Phil tried to avoid eye contact with Benny, rain slick over his bald head. A triple strobe flash of lightning froze the scene into a succession of tableaux, followed by another concussive blast of thunder rolling over the trees and a sudden downpour of rain.

"Get out of the car, Phil!" Benny roared through the increasing rain. "Get out here! Now!"

Phil sat with a rigid back staring straight ahead through the windshield. Benny's rage fed on his impatience as Phil took three deep breaths, each lasting moments upon moments. With fear and shame weighing down his visage, Phil turned and faced Benny through the bit of protection offered by the rolled up window.

Phil pushed open his door, like a timid child approaching for punishment. The rusted hinges complained with creaks and pops. Rain soaked down Phil's hair and ran down his face. His tears lost in the wet cold.

Not yelling, but speaking above the din of the skidder and the downpour, "I loved your daughter." He continued his slow approach, eyes now locked on Benny's.

The barn owl flew out of the woods and

circled overhead, watching. Witnessing. Waiting. Behavior more vulture-like than owl.

Once Phil was far enough away from the truck for Benny's liking, Benny sprinted at Phil and landed a heavy right punch into the side of Phil's head; still holding the axe tight with his left grip. "Why didn't he go after you instead?" Benny yelled as Phil fell to the ground, holding a hand over a bloodied cheekbone. "Why weren't you there to stop him?!"

Benny stood over his prey, lightning ripped through the sky; the owl continued to circle above. Thick rivulets of blood ran down the side of Phil's head and onto the muddied ground.

Spittle flew from Benny's lips, "You didn't deserve her, you damned greenhorn! I took you in, trained you!"

Phil cowered below Benny's bestial rage. "She didn't want to stay here!" His voice cracked like a teenage boy, mid sob.

Benny's eyes flicked wide and his deep uncontrolled breathing froze.

"We were saving up to move East. It was her idea…"

"Tom was right! You were gonna take her away from me!" Benny drove the sharpened points of his left boot into Phil's bicep, pinning the arm to the ground. Gouts of blood flowed into the surrounding mud. The ground drank it in as Phil screamed, eyes wide with pain and shock as he tried to push Benny's leg up and off of him with both hands. Benny worried that Frankie and Buster might hear, but fresh thunder masked the screams.

Benny stared down at his cutting partner, writhing beneath him, his body surrounded in a halo of red-stained mud. He lifted the axe, ready to split Phil's skull. He didn't see Phil's hand reaching for his right boot. The barn owl screeched as it swooped down towards Benny's head. With a screaming grunt, Phil threw Benny off balance, tossing him on his back on top of the sharp gravel. The axe landed in the muddy drainage along the upslope side of the road.

Roles reversed, Phil stood over Benny, blood still running down and masking half of his face, "What did this place have for her? Nothing! Did you really expect her to waste away at that diner? She loved you! More than anything. She just wanted something… anything more!" His voice wavered as he worked to remain conscious. "We were going to tell you. I wanted to tell you." With those wavering words he fell to the ground, unconscious from from blood loss. Benny's body was overtaken with convulsive sobbing as he wailed into the storm, a scream filled with grief and remorse. Pushing out every last bit of air from his lungs to grieve his daughter's loss as if freshly reported to him at his screen door.

"Oi! What's going on?" Buster yelled from up the road, fists on his hips, orange hard hat on his head. Frankie ran over the ridge behind him. They both looked confused, mouths hanging open.

Benny did not reply and both sprinted toward the scene.

"What the fuck happened here?" Asked Buster, out of breath.

"Looks like Benny messed that boy up!" said Frankie, running up beside Buster.

"You do this, Benny?" asked Buster, disappointment in his gaze. He already knew the answer, but he'd started to help him up. Benny nodded and Buster loosened his grip, letting Benny fall back to the road. "You can help yourself up," said Buster shaking his head and turning his back to Benny.

"I'll go back up for the truck, we need to get

this kid to the hospital," said Frankie, before running back up the road.

Minutes later he was back with Buster's rusted out red International Diesel. They loaded Phil into the center of the bench seat. Buster took the wheel. Frankie slipped into the passenger side and propped Phil up on his shoulder, not caring about the blood. Before Buster gunned the engine Frankie rolled down the window, "I'll be sending the sheriff up this way." Frankie gave Benny a long questioning look. "I know you'll do the right thing. Just you wait here and fess up. You're a better man than all of this." Frankie let out a sigh then rolled the window up and they drove the rattling truck down the road and past the empty snag.

The rain soaked through to his skin as Benny remained seated in the middle of the forestry road waiting for the sheriff. He entertained the thought of running only for a few seconds before he settled in and accepted his fate. Where would he go? What would he do? There was nowhere and nothing.

Lightning continued to rip the sky to shreds. He wanted his daughter back. He wanted his wife back. He wanted to not be alone in his rotting mobile home. He wanted everything to end.

He was about to lay back down when a small owl with Adrianna's face landed beside him, this one a brown spotted owl. Her face was not stapled at the edges to the tiny animal's head, as Tom's had been to the cat's. Instead, it was trimmed and neatly tucked into the edges of the feathers framing, what should have been, the owl's face. A purple plastic seagull barrette held back a tuft of feathers on one side.

She stood less than a foot tall in the gravel beside him, tilting her head side to side in a questioning, yet very much owlish, way. Her eyes had expansive abyssal pupils. She looked into his eyes, her gold ring irises constricting and expanding around the black center.

"I am so sorry," tears flowed and mixed with the rain running down his face. "I should've been there for you. I should've sat down spoke with you, asked you what you wanted out of all of this," he motioned with a wave of his hand, encompassing everything that had made up their lives, including the little town at the bottom of the forestry road. "I should've let you move on."

The owl tilted its head with a quizzical look,

its face rigid, blank. The owl-eyes quietly taking in everything.

"I can't handle being alone. But it isn't right, expecting you to rot away out here." He rolled to get up. "I'm done holding you back, Adrianna. I want you to move on and I'll do my best to do the same. Somehow, I'll figure things out." Benny said to the Adrianna-owl, shooing her away with both hands. "Go and be free of me", he cried but forced a smile for her. The owl tilted its head to the other side, took flight, and circled high above. She arched out over the deep valley and back to the trees on the upslope, before disappearing into the forest.

Benny decided to go down to the bottom of the forest road and meet the sheriff there. He was ready to turn himself in. He knew he could not yet face Phil, but, in time, he would apologize.

He left his axe on the side of the road, the mud slowly burying it. Sitting in the driver's seat, he pulled off the cork boots and threw them in the back. He did not bother to put on his driving shoes and reached across the sopping passenger seat to pull the door closed before starting the old blue truck.

The dry-rotted wipers could not keep up with

rain, which had increased to a downpour, falling in sheets. He couldn't see more than twenty feet ahead. Yet, after a three,four,five-point turn, he was able to aim the truck back down the forestry road.

As he approached the narrow portion of the road between the snag and the valley below, a flash of lightning streaked across his vision, revealing the silhouette of the barn owl back at its vigil on top of the snag. The headlights were not enough to penetrate the increasing rain. Benny did not see the freshly washed-out road in time. He rolled the truck along slowly, but the front tires went over the edge, followed by the back tires, though the time between felt like an eternity of regret.

The owl watched the truck as it tipped downward and rolled along with the rushing water of the washout. The truck flipped end-over-end as it descended deeper and deeper into the storm-darkened valley. It could see the truck on the first, second, but not the third lightning strike over the valley.

Later, before the sheriff arrived, the rain stopped. The clouds brightened, and blue sky broke through. The valley below was lit and saturated with intense color, only ever present after a substantial storm. The air was cleansed of smoke and dust. The spotted owl returned from the trees and circled above the barn owl on its snag.

The barn owl gave up its vigil.

Together they flew into the forest, leaving the valley and the mangled truck behind.

AUTHOR ACKNOWLEGMENTS

First of all, I must thank my wife, Melissa and my son for putting up with my varying creative itches over the years. Melissa has supported me every step of the way, and I wouldn't be the person I am today without her. Next, I must thank the amazing Leo for all of his hard work. I first met him at an art show back in the 2010s in Chickasha, Oklahoma. His work was so much darker than what I was used to seeing in small town USA, and I loved it. It reminded me of the different creatures in the horror stories I loved to read. We kept in touch over the years, and this book is the fruit of our friendship. I look forward to working with Leo on future projects. Then, there is my writing critique group. We call ourselves the Write Club (so don't ask any questions) and we meet virtually twice a month to workshop each others' writing. This story would not be where it is today if it weren't for the valuable feedback from Tori Fredrick, Brian Noonan,

Jon Shank, Pam Durgin, and Alex Langer. Then, there is my local writing "support" group. This includes Hardcore Mango, David Beaumier, Leslie Copeland, Mike Ramos, Rayviathae, and others. Many thanks to awesome folks who are there to commiserate with me as we beat our heads against our keyboards. And finally, I have to call out my Mom and Dad, Kristina and Howard Donley, for always cheering my every success, no matter how small.

—Joe

STORY NOTES

If you haven't noticed, I'm a touch obsessed with the Olympic Peninsula, a landmass approximately the size of Massachusetts filled with snow-capped peaks, old growth rainforests, and rugged coast-lines. This is a perfect setting for a horror story, don't you think? Surprisingly, this is not my first story about cats with human faces who also live in the wilds of Washington State. No, the first was a story called 'The Cutter's Daughter', published in anthology with a very small print run. This newer story was originally meant to explain where these horrifying cats come from, though, I'm not sure anyone would truly want to know.

—Joe

ILLUSTRATION NOTES

It took quite a bit of research to find out how I should approach illustrating a real location I have never visited. I had to gather as many high-quality reference images of the rainforest as I could. I had to convince the reader that this was the Hoh Rainforest. The sheer array of tentacular roots, sword ferns, twisting vines, hanging moss, lichen-covered rocks, and general visual overload of this rainforest is staggering. It was tricky, but I feel that I managed to come up with a balanced composition that communicates that intense detail without sacrificing aesthetic harmony.

The witch was fun to design. She is approach-able, but in a way that lacks all warmth. Behind

her deep, hooded black eyes and her chipper atti-
tude, lies nothing but malice, and a desire to cause
pain.

—Leo

ABOUT THE AUTHOR

J. W. Donley

JW lives with his wife and son in the Pacific Northwest where the Cascade Mountains meet the Salish Sea. He enjoys writing in the weird, horror, and fantasy genres.

Growing up he enjoyed R. L. Stine's *Goosebumps* books as well as classics like *Dune*, and *Lord of the Rings*. Later he discovered Mark Danielewski's *House of Leaves* and authors like Clive Barker and Laird Barron.

JW's short stories have appeared in anthologies from PIT, Dim Shores, and HOWL Society Press.

JW also does custom cover design and book formatting as a service. If you need any of these services please reach out!

Visit JW on the web at: JWDonley.com

instagram.com/jw_donley
facebook.com/jdonley83
goodreads.com/jwdonley

ABOUT THE ILLUSTRATOR

Leo Corbett

Leo lives and works in Oklahoma City. He attended local schools and the University of Science and Arts of Oklahoma, graduating with a Bachelor of Fine Arts degree. It is here he began his association with Joe Donley.

His early inspirations included the *Star Wars* films, *Batman: Mask of the Phantasm,* as well as Stephen Gammell's striking illustrations for *Scary Stories to Tell in the Dark.* He later discovered the work of concept artist Doug Chiang, world famous American artist Burne Hogarth, and the psychedelic chaos of French comic creator Phillippe Druilet.

Cats of the Pacific Northwest is the first time his illustrations have appeared in a published work.

Find Leo at his website: https://lcor7601.wixsite.com/website

CONTENT WARNINGS

blood, gore, death, murder, misogyny, animal cruelty

www.ingramcontent.com/pod-product-compliance
Lightning Source LLC
Chambersburg PA
CBHW021022160726
47994CB00006B/2621